Let's Go to the Library!

by Charles M. Schulz

Adapted by May Nakamura • Illustrated by Robert Pope

Ready-to-Read

Simon Spotlight

New York   London   Toronto   Sydney   New Delhi

SIMON SPOTLIGHT

An imprint of Simon & Schuster Children's Publishing Division
1230 Avenue of the Americas, New York, New York 10020
This Simon Spotlight edition August 2020
© 2020 Peanuts Worldwide LLC
For information about special discounts for bulk purchases,
please contact Simon & Schuster Special Sales at 1-866-506-1949 or
business@simonandschuster.com.
Manufactured in the United States of America 0720 LAK
2 4 6 8 10 9 7 5 3 1
ISBN 978-1-5344-6957-0 (hc)
ISBN 978-1-5344-6956-3 (pbk)
ISBN 978-1-5344-6958-7 (eBook)

It was a special day
for Sally Brown.
She was getting her
very first library card!

Sally and her big brother,
Charlie Brown,
walked to the library.
Linus, Sally's Sweet Babboo,
joined them.

Sally was so happy
that her Sweet Babboo
was coming along
on her special day!

Soon they reached the library.
Sally started feeling nervous.
"I've never been inside a library
before," she said.

"This will be a good experience for you," Charlie Brown replied. "I think everyone should get to know their librarian."

Sally took a deep breath
and walked to the librarian's desk.

She looked up.
"*Know* their librarian?" she said.
"I can't even *see* the librarian!"

The librarian gave Sally
a plastic card.
Sally carefully wrote her name
on the back, and . . .

Ta-da!
She now had her own library card!
"That was easy," she said.

Linus, Sally, and Charlie Brown
wandered around the library.
It was full of people.

"You can do many things
at the library,"
Charlie Brown said.
He pointed to
Peppermint Patty and Marcie,
who were doing their homework.

Peppermint Patty wanted to
go outside and play baseball.
"No games until you finish
your book report," Marcie said.

Then Lucy walked by.
"I can't believe it!"
she yelled at Charlie Brown.
"You missed
my book club meeting!"

"Good grief,"
Charlie Brown replied.
"I didn't even know
you *had* a book club!"
"Shh! Use your quiet voices
in the library," Linus warned.

A few minutes later Sally spotted
Snoopy and Woodstock
doing a puzzle.

"I didn't know dogs were allowed
in the library," she said.
This dog is! Snoopy thought.

"Come on, Sally. Let's find
a book for you to check out,"
Charlie Brown said.

They walked up and down the
aisles.
There were so many books
to choose from!

Sally found a book
with many pictures inside.
"Now take this book to
the librarian," Charlie Brown said.
"Tell her you'd like to borrow it."

"But I don't have any money!"
Sally cried.

"You don't need any money,"
Linus replied.

"Really?"
Sally thought about that
for a moment.
Then she declared,
"Libraries are *wonderful*!"

Sally brought the book
and her library card
to the checkout desk.
The librarian scanned the card
and the book with a machine.
Then she gave Sally a paper slip
printed with the book's due date.

CHECK

After saying goodbye
to their friends,
Sally and Charlie Brown
left the library.

At home Sally settled
into her beanbag
and started reading.

She didn't look up until
the end of the book!

Sally turned to her brother,
who was reading his own book.
"I learned something
very important today,"
she said.

"What is that?"
asked Charlie Brown.

Sally smiled. "Happiness is having your own library card!"